Draw close, children, and I will weave you a tale.

Toys can be fun. But a good story is magic. And there is no better time for one than when rain is tapping at your window.

Know this, though, children: Stories are like the skies. They can change, bring surprises, catch you without a coat.

Look up all you want, but you never really know what's coming.

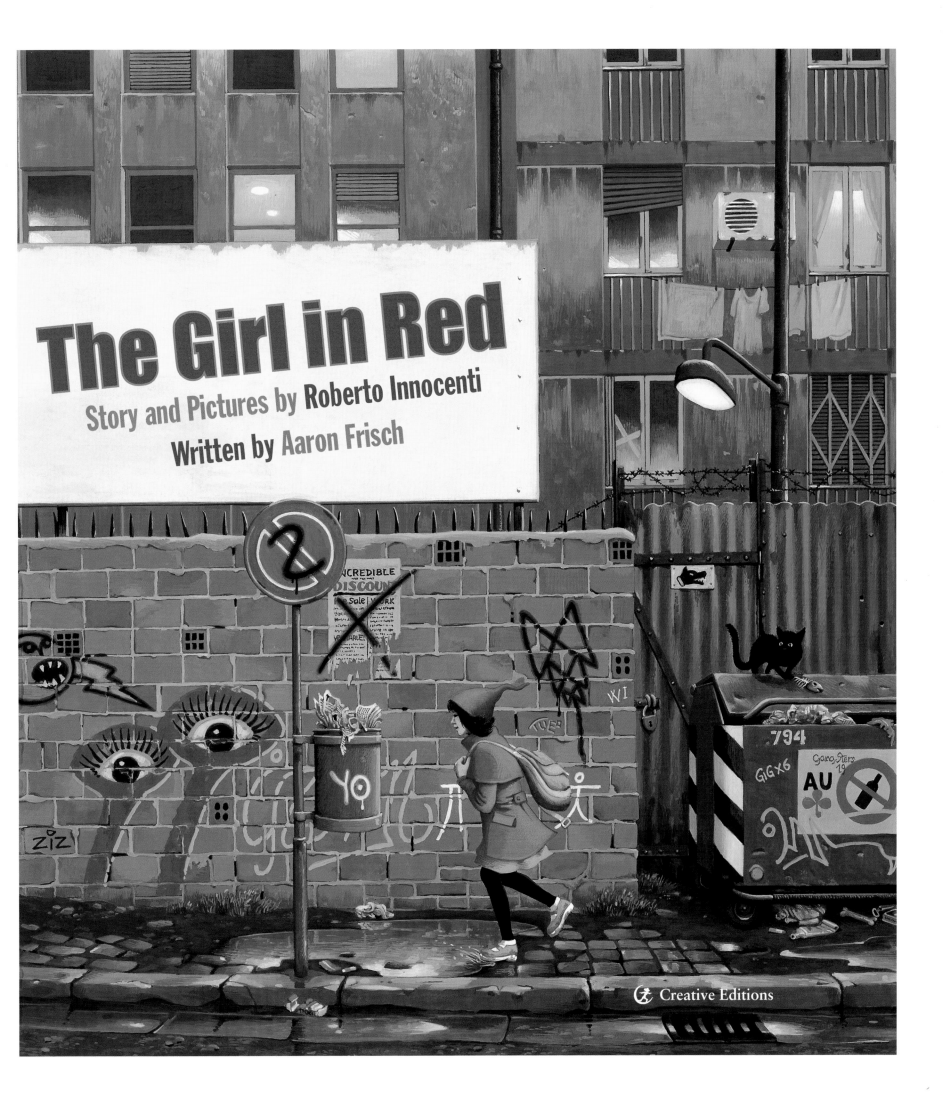

Our story takes place in a forest.

This forest has few trunks and leaves—it is composed of concrete and bricks instead.

In the day, and especially in good light, the dwellers live contentedly enough, to each their own.

Among them, at the edge of the forest, is a quiet girl named Sophia.

Sophia lives with her mother and sister. Her grandmother lives on the other side of the forest. Nana is feeling poorly again. She could use company.

Sophia fills her pack with biscuits, honey, and oranges. She buttons her hooded coat—the one Nana made for her. The forecast is for variable weather.

The walk is long, but Sophia is a good girl.

Sophia hears the echoes of her footsteps. She hears, too, her mother's words: Stay on the main trail all the way.

Outside, the forest is big.

Sophia is young, still learning the ways of the wilderness. She is learning that large numbers on the main trail can mean safety.

But always, you must keep your ears up.

Everyone sees you, but no one does.

Sophia walks and takes in the forest's wonderments.

Music.

Magic.

Mysteries.

And then Sophia reaches the greatest wonderment of all.
The heart of the forest.

It is a place everyone calls "The Wood."

Almost anything you want can be had here.

The heart of the forest, though, can be very dark.
Especially when storm clouds roll.

The Wood is full of color, noise, and temptations.

It is a world unto itself.

Sophia thinks of her mother's words and hurries through.

She hurries, but already she can picture her favorite display.

And then she sees it.

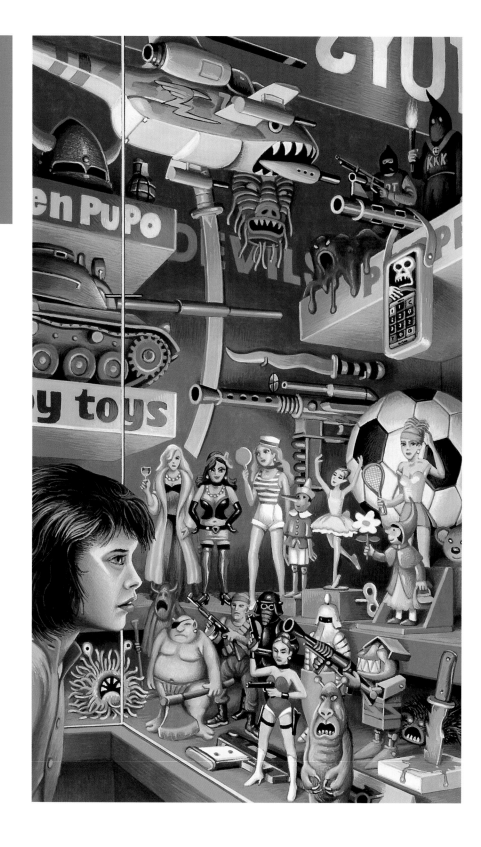

The window of wonders. Sophia stops and gets to dreaming. Before her are monsters, princesses, dark fates, and happily-ever-afters. Images of the past and of the future.

Sophia longs to linger, but she feels the weight of her pack. She can dawdle no more. She looks for her exit.

The Wood, though, has many exits, leading every which way. Sophia does not know this part of the forest.

The trail is lost.

Another thing about the forest: Empty paths are never truly empty. Always there are eyes watching, noses sniffing for an advantage. The forest has many jackals. Alone, they are cowardly …

… but they grow bold in numbers.

The rain falls hard.

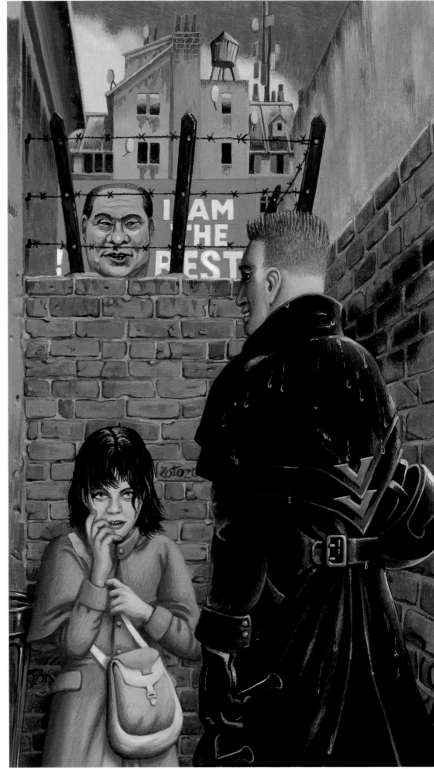

Suddenly, lightning splits the sky.

In the wildest parts of the forest, the law of the food chain holds sway. Small creatures give way to large ones. With a clap of thunder, the jackals are gone.

A smiling hunter. What big teeth he has. Dark and strong and perfect in his timing. Sophia tells him of her grandmother and her little home. Of the biscuits and honey.

The hunter knows the forest well, he assures Sophia.

They will reach Nana quickly, he promises.

The sun peeks out.

The hunter's phone rings. He is sorry but can go no farther.

He has urgent business now.

Nana is close, at least.

But not too close.

The sky growls again.

Sophia begins to run.

Nana is not at the door, as she usually is.

Sophia calls for her.

Darkness falls.

All goes black but for one apartment.

What keen ears wolves have. What sharp noses.

Across the forest, a shadow creeps just ahead of the sirens and lights.

Police arrive, armed to the teeth.

But the hour is late.

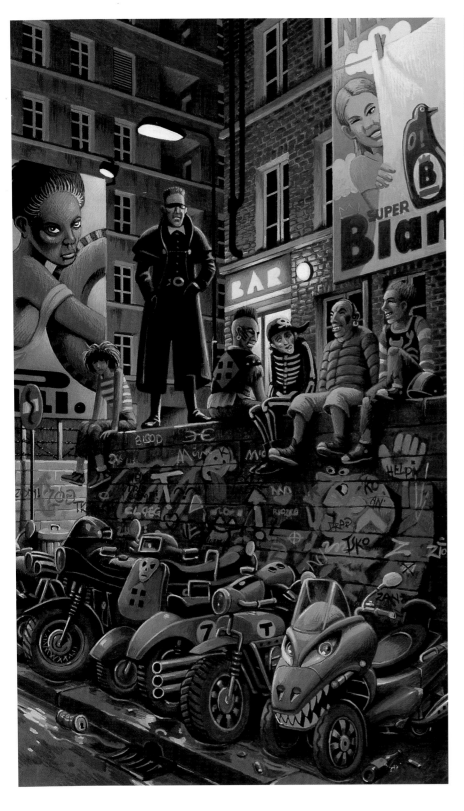

The truth is that wolves and jackals are not so different.
They have the same wicked grins. It is only size that
separates them.

It is almost morning when a mother's phone rings.

The clouds will allow no sun today.

Now, children, do not be ashamed of your tears!
They are as natural as the rain. But they are not
necessary here.

Remember the thing about stories? Stories are magic.
Who says they can have only one ending?

Picture this instead, if you like.

A woodcutter sees a wolf prowling about a home. He makes a call. The police are fast to appear, swooping in with the setting sun.

The wolf is snared; a family is spared.

The stars will shine on the forest tonight.

Library of Congress Cataloging-in-Publication Data
Frisch, Aaron.
The girl in red / written by Aaron Frisch; illustrated by Roberto Innocenti.
Summary: The illustrations of award-winning artist Roberto Innocenti
offer a modern take on the centuries-old tale of an innocent girl in a red
riding hood who meets a wicked wolf in the dark woods.
ISBN 978-1-56846-223-3
[1. Fairy tales. 2. Folklore.] I. Innocenti, Roberto, ill. II. Little Red Riding
Hood. English. III. Title.
PZ8.F9144Gi 2012
398.2—dc23   2011044745
First edition   9 8 7 6 5 4 3 2 1